Mother Goose

Nursery Rhymes

illustrated by Cristina Ong

What are little girls made of, made of,
What are little girls made of?
Sugar and spice, and all things that are nice;
And that's what little girls are made of, made of.

What are little boys made of, made of,
What are little boys made of?
Snaps and snails, and puppy-dogs tails;
And that's what little boys are made of, made of.

Here we go round the mulberry bush,
The mulberry bush, the mulberry bush,
Here we go round the mulberry bush.
On a cold and frosty morning.

Ring a ring o' roses,
A pocketful of posies.
Tisha! Tisha!
We all fall down.

Jack and Jill went up the hill,
To fetch a pail of water;
Jack fell down, and broke his crown,
And Jill came tumbling after.

Mary had a little lamb,
Its fleece was white as snow;
And everywhere that Mary went
The lamb was sure to go.
He followed her to school one day —
That was against the rule;
It made the children laugh and play
To see a lamb at school.

The rose is red; the violet's blue,
Honey's sweet; and so are you.
Thou art my love, and I am thine,
I drew thee for my Valentine;
The lot was cast, and then I drew.
And fortune said it should be you.

Pat-a-cake, pat-a-cake, baker's man;
So I will, master, as fast as I can:
Pat it, and prick it, and mark it with B,
Put it in the oven for Baby and me.

Mary, Mary, quite contrary,
How does your garden grow?
Silver bells and cockle-shells,
And pretty maids all of a row.

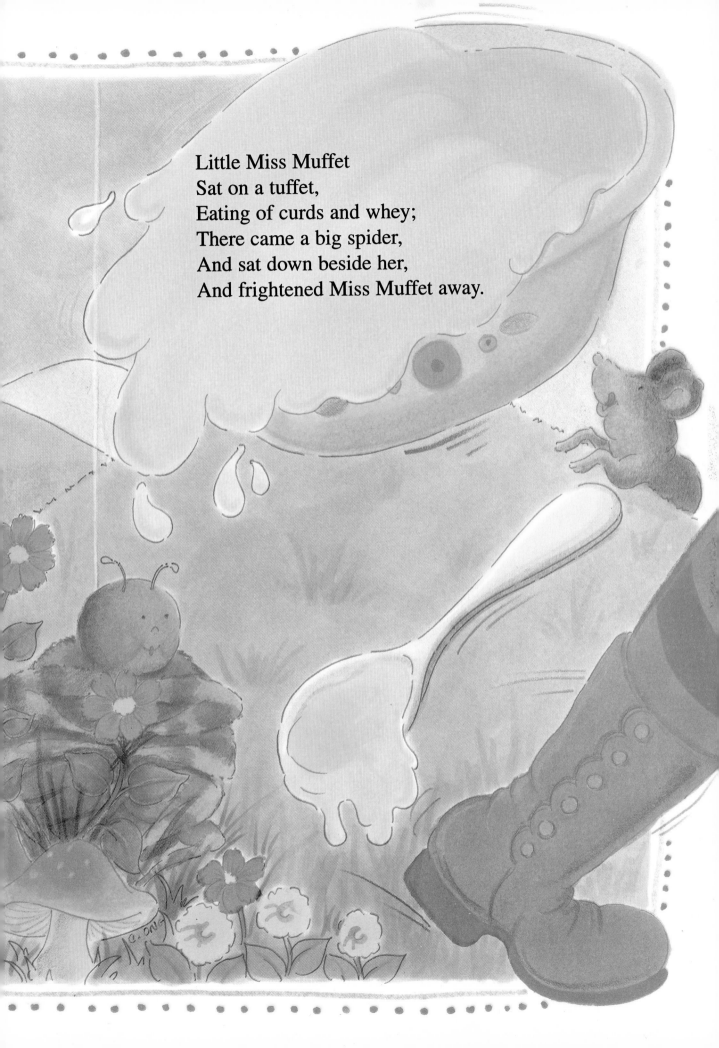

Little Miss Muffet
Sat on a tuffet,
Eating of curds and whey;
There came a big spider,
And sat down beside her,
And frightened Miss Muffet away.

Polly, put the kettle on,
Polly, put the kettle on,
Polly, put the kettle on,
And let's drink tea.

Sukey, take it off again,
Sukey, take it off again,
Sukey, take it off again,
They're all gone away.

Bye, baby bunting,
Father's gone a-hunting,
Mother's gone a-milking,
Sister's gone a-silking,
And brother's gone to buy a skin
To wrap the baby bunting in.

Jack be nimble,
Jack be quick,
Jack jump over
The candlestick.

Star light, star bright,
First star I see to-night,
I wish I may, I wish I might
Have the wish I wish to-night.